MAGGIE AND THE BLACK-TIE AFFAIR

A CARITA COVE ROMANTIC MYSTERY

BARBARA COOL LEE

PAJARO BAY PUBLISHING

INTRODUCTION

Maggie and the Black-Tie Affair is a pint-sized story introducing you to the new Carita Cove romantic mystery series:

A bored trophy wife. A cynical movie star. One evening to save an innocent girl from prison. None of them will ever be the same after this Black-Tie Affair.

Carita Cove romantic mysteries are fun and flirty reads, with no swearing or love scenes, and no gruesome violence to keep you up at night. Collect them all:

- 1. Maggie and the Black-Tie Affair (short intro story)
- 2. Maggie and the Inconvenient Corpse
- 3. Maggie and the Mourning Beads
- 4. Maggie and the Empty Noose
- 5. Maggie and the Huichol Homicide
- 6. Maggie and the Whiskered Witness
- And more to come.

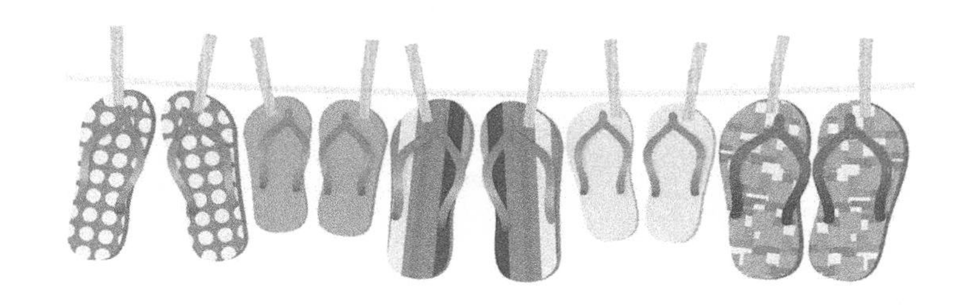

**Sign up for
Barbara Cool Lee's
email newsletter list
to get free stories &
new release alerts:**

http://BarbaraCoolLee.com

This is a work of fiction. Names, characters, places, and incidents either are the products of the author's imagination or are used fictitiously. Any resemblance to actual persons, living or dead, businesses, companies, events, or locales is entirely coincidental.

Neither the author nor the publisher claim responsibility for adverse effects resulting from the use of any recipes, projects, and/or information found within this book.

This edition published: October 22, 2019

First Edition.

2019-10-15-Aa

As always, for Mom,
my co-writer.

http://barbaracoollee.com

MAGGIE AND THE BLACK-TIE AFFAIR

December 31, Late Evening
Carita, California

The ritzy New Year's Eve party was in full swing at *Casablanca,* Michael "Big Mac" McJasper's beach house in the coastal town of Carita, California.

Magdalena Lopez McJasper, known to all as Maggie, glanced surreptitiously at a clock. Just a few more hours and she would finally get to celebrate the new year the way she wanted to:

She would peel off the belly-squashing Spanx that were the only thing keeping her sparkling silver Jenny Packham gown from bursting at the seams.

She would remove the acrylic nails that were already sporting a big chip that snagged on everything she touched.

She would put on her sweats, sit out by the pool in the moonlight, and start that last Agatha Christie novel on her ereader.

And she would eat. After starving herself to fit into this dress, she was famished.

But all that was still hours away.

So Maggie surveyed the room instead, watching for anywhere things might be lagging and need a hostess's deft touch to keep the energy going.

The party was made up of the same cliquish little group of actors, directors, models, agents, hangers-on, and sycophants as always. An exclusive party, small enough for guests to feel flattered to be invited, yet not so small that they couldn't make connections.

They all milled around in the huge, high-ceilinged living room of Casablanca, with its view out the glowing windows to the blue-lit waterfall pool and the gigantic rusting wave sculpture by a famous artist, to the endless sky and water of Carita Cove beyond.

But no one glanced out the windows. They were

focused instead on their fellow lucky insiders, and the deals to be made.

She smiled automatically when anyone glanced her way.

She knew most of the guests, but didn't really *know* any of them. Did that model miss her family in Belgrade? Did that director ever wish he'd chosen a different career? Did that agent really intend for his hair to look like that?

She mingled, and made sure everyone had champagne, and chatted amiably, as was her job at these events. They had the same conversations about the same narrow list of subjects, and everyone judged everyone else's appearance, financial status, and (most importantly for this crowd) their position on the pyramid of Hollywood power.

And here came someone at the top of that pyramid. Reese Stevens had shown up, with the latest pretty actress/model on his arm. All heads turned.

Or actually, they didn't. Everyone oh-so-casually glanced in his direction, and then went back to whatever they were doing. But she knew they were all watching out of the corners of their eyes, hoping for that chance to, in a very cool and unstudied way, strike up a conversation with the studio's number one box office star.

Her husband commanded that same kind of attention, though for a very different reason. Her dear husband Mac was not, unfortunately, a six-foot-three and drop-dead gorgeous blond movie star. He was middle-aged, and his scalp had only recently healed from getting hair plugs to cover the bald spots.

But her Mac could work a room with the same charm that had captured her attention all those years ago. He was in great shape from his daily laps in the pool, and she still thought he was an attractive man, in a more *regular guy with a good tailor* way.

But to this crowd, Mac's star quality rivaled Reese's, because he was a producer at a prestigious boutique film studio, a behind-the-scenes executive who had launched a dozen careers.

So everyone wanted to close a deal with Big Mac.

And so they were nice to her.

Maggie excused herself from a scintillating conversation about retail receipt calculations between a studio accountant and an aspiring actor who was making a heroic effort to not yawn, and wandered over to the buffet, which had been set up by the massive stone living room fireplace.

A bit too close to the fireplace.

She pointed out to the caterer that the chocolate cake was melting, and the staff scrambled to move the buffet out of harm's way. She resisted the urge to help them. Mac hated when she acted *déclassé,* as he called it.

She called it treating staff like human beings, but Mac didn't agree. The staff should be invisible, and she should be visible.

So she didn't offer to help the group of college kids and locals who moonlighted at these fancy parties to make ends meet in Carita. She just smiled at them, and turned away from the efforts to rescue the gourmet meal.

No dinner for her tonight. Her best friend Brooke was home in her pajamas, eating pizza and binge-watching *Buffy the Vampire Slayer*. But Brooke didn't have a husband who considered every holiday a chance to further his career—and who considered his wife an important part of the scene decoration for this little staged event.

So Maggie just stood there, the firelight making her silver evening gown sparkle, wearing diamond earrings the size of chandeliers (a guilt present from Mac the last time he'd been out of the country micromanaging some over-budget production), and wishing she hadn't chosen the silver Manolo pumps that pinched her toes, and hoping there would be some cake left when this was done.

And she was over it.

Over the whole thing.

The party.

The shallow people (none of whom would even speak to her if she weren't married to a big shot).

The prime rib (that the men were devouring and none of the women were touching, lest their own evening gowns end up too small).

The house—

No. She stopped herself there. She wasn't over the house.

She loved this house. She actually loved this house best of all their houses. She had redecorated it herself when Mac had decided he wanted to spend more time in Carita, the self-proclaimed Playground of the Stars a few hours from LA. The town prided itself on its down-to-earth, funky beach-town vibe (while being in reality one of the most expensive places in California, thus keeping out the riffraff).

She loved Carita. She loved the little downtown with its coffee shops and boutiques. She loved *The Row*, the exclusive street of oceanfront houses that stretched along the sandy beach like a pearl necklace.

And Casablanca was right in the center of the necklace, in the prime spot where the curve of the cove had deposited the golden sand at their feet.

She loved this house overlooking the sea. She loved the small-town escape from LA's fussy, empty lifestyle of spas and shopping and dinner parties where everyone jockeyed to get closer to the centers of power.

Her husband was one of those centers of power, being a producer of films that earned the studio a fortune and made actors into household names.

But she? Where did she fit into this perfect fairy tale?

Reese Stevens and his latest date, a truly lovely young woman who had clearly not eaten chocolate cake in years, were talking to the droning accountant now. Presumably he was still regaling them with his theories on net versus gross tax bases.

The woman was skinny as a rail, with bolt-ons and a mane of toffee-colored hair. Every time she tossed her hair back and laughed, her earrings glittered.

Now that they were closer, Maggie recognized the earrings. They were a pair of absolutely stunning

Miyamotos in the Waterwheel design, worth a solid 250K.

The woman also sported a simple diamond ring, which Maggie was happy to see was not on her engagement finger. She knew Reese slightly from his attendance at all Mac's parties, and she somehow couldn't imagine him dating an engaged woman. Or, even worse, proposing to one whose voice, now that Maggie could hear her, sounded exactly like fingernails scraping across a blackboard.

Maggie tuned out the sound and focused on the earrings.

The waterwheel effect was beautiful. There was a little diamond-studded hoop at the top of each earring, then white gold chains, also studded with diamonds, fell down like water drops, each ending in one of the stunning pearls for which Miyamoto was justifiably famous.

Her fingers itched to get to her craft table and try something out. What if she reversed the design, putting big faux pearls at the top of the earring, instead of the bottom? Changed up the color, using her favorite velvety purple glass pearl instead of a real one? And what if she created a swirl of tiny beads hanging from the center, instead of platinum chains attached around the outside?

The resulting earrings would be completely different from the Miyamotos. They would have a similar whispering movement every time she turned her head, but they would be crafted from little glass beads in a rainbow of colors, and would be anchored by silky purple faux pearls instead of quite real and quite priceless gems.

If she used sterling silver components to hold them together, they would even match the silver evening gown she was wearing.

Then she deflated. Mac would never let her wear homemade earrings to a party like this. But she could still make them, and maybe wear them when he was out of town. Or she could give them to a friend. They would be fun to create, anyway.

Mac never understood why she didn't just use the Black AmEx card he provided to buy whatever she wanted, instead of creating things from scratch. But maybe that was because he didn't feel as useless as a pretty vase sitting on a shelf, the way she often did.

She smiled to herself. Her earrings would cost less than ten dollars, would be completely different from the ones the girl was wearing, and yet she would love them more than the designer ones. They would be her own creation, something she thought of herself, then brought to life with needle and thread.

"Are you jealous?" the nasally voice said.

Maggie realized she was still staring at the woman's earrings. "Sorry," she replied. "I was just admiring your Miyamotos."

The girl examined Maggie from head to toe, then dismissed her as unimportant. "Too expensive for you, honey. You're too old to get a man to give them to you."

Wow. Great manners on this girl. Maggie bit back a retort. This was a business event, despite all the trappings of a festive party, and she didn't want to cause a scene that could disrupt all the wheeling and dealing her husband was doing here tonight.

Reese strolled up, a glass of orange juice in his hand. He came within earshot just in time to hear Maggie say, "I'm only about a decade older than you. And believe me, kid, those years are gonna go by fast."

"You wear it well," Reese said to her. "I'm so glad you didn't wreck your face with fillers and lip boosters."

She raised an eyebrow at him. "Is that sarcasm because you can see my wrinkles under these lights?"

"No," he said. "It's not. I'm not always sarcastic, you know."

"I didn't know," she replied.

"So where's Big Mac?"

"On an important call. The Chinese distributor for that post-apocalypse film is having some sort of crisis."

He rolled his eyes. "Aren't they always?"

The girl on his arm whined, clearly not happy that he was talking to a thirty-something brunette whose hips were larger than her waist. She whispered something to him, the last part of which sounded like "liposuction."

Reese smirked, and then, with the sweet smile that had broken a million hearts onscreen, said, "I forgot to introduce you. This is Maggie McJasper, your hostess."

His date went pale under her spray-on tan. "I'm so happy to meet you," she said swiftly.

"I'm sure you are," Maggie said. "And your name is...?"

"Oh, sorry," Reese said. "This is...."

Then he stopped. He turned to the woman clutching his arm, and with a quizzical expression, asked innocently, "what was your name?"

"Felicia Dalton," she said.

"Right," he said blandly. He turned back to Maggie and winked. "Maggie, this is Telisha Malton."

"It's nice to meet you," she said. "Excuse me while I check on my guests."

She left them there. She knew Felicia would forgive Reese. It would be hard not to, with those chiseled features and the cobalt blue eyes that were his trademark.

But even if he'd been downright ugly, no ambitious actress would dare to be offended by Reese Stevens. He was her ticket to this party, and so anything he said would be forgiven.

She often got the impression he pushed the limits of people's tolerance of him just to see how fake they were. Most were fake. Most everyone at this party was. She'd seen it herself. She was a beloved part of this little insular community, just as long as she was married to Big Mac McJasper. If she ever left him (and let's just say the bloom was off that particular rose), she too would find out who was only faking friendship pretty quickly.

She scanned the room. It hadn't been that long ago when Mac would have been right by her side, proud and happy, attentive and loving. But she had felt him drifting away for a while now. She'd even suggested the couples therapy that Nora swore had saved her marriage. He had put her off with a distracted, "maybe after the first of the year."

Their tenth anniversary was coming up after the first of the year. It was hard to believe that was possible. Where had the time gone?

SHE WANDERED OUT ONTO THE PATIO.

She stood out there for a long time, working up the nerve to go back and face the party.

"Champagne?"

She turned around to see Reese offering her a crystal flute.

She smiled. "You don't need to give me your champagne."

"Yes, I do." He held it out to her, and she took it. "Some idiot stuck it in my hand and I need to dump it before a paparazzo with a telephoto lens gets the money shot of me drinking."

"Of course." His hard-won sobriety was part of his fame. And more importantly, he couldn't get film roles without artist liability insurance, and that meant proving he was staying sober.

She took a sip. "It's gone flat."

She set it on the rim of a potted plant. "I'd actually rather have a cup of coffee."

"Me, too," he said. "I've been guzzling orange juice. I'm sick of sparkling water. Why can't these parties ever have enough non-booze options?"

"Sorry," she said. "I'll talk to the caterer about it before next time."

"Don't worry. I'm just whining. It's a great party."

"Sure," she said.

"I can think of worse places to spend tonight," he said.

"I'm sure you can."

The moon shone down on them on this clear evening, making the pool glimmer like diamonds.

"Gorgeous, isn't it?" she said.

"Yeah. I'm sure Big Mac paid NASA a bonus to get the moonlight just right."

She laughed.

They both stared at the rusting iron wave sculpture that towered over the pool like a deranged vulture.

"No offense, Maggie, but that thing is just plain ugly."

"It's famous. Or something. It came with the house and now I can't figure out how to get rid of it without offending the art world."

They listened to it rattle in the breeze.

"Hey," he said softly. "About what I said back there—I'm sorry if my fillers comment was rude."

"Don't worry about it."

"I was just mad at Felicia and it came out wrong."

"I'm not offended, really. I got it."

"I actually meant you look very pretty. I don't dare have fillers myself, and I'm older than you. There's only so much Botox you can inject before you become a cartoon."

"Especially as an actor," she said.

"Exactly. After a while your face gets that frozen expression and you can't do the job."

"Especially in high def," she agreed.

"Yeah. The close ups are brutal. If you're a man, the age lines give you character. If you're a woman, you're just old and ready to be traded in on a new model."

She gave him a baleful look. "Thanks a lot."

"Don't mention it," he said with a grin. "I haven't had an on-screen love interest in my age range since I was twenty-five."

"Or off-screen."

"Touché."

"I get it," she said. "This is the world we live in.

My husband hired a twenty-three-year-old to play a teen's mother in his latest movie."

"Ah. You saw the rushes of Mac's new family-friendly blockbuster."

"I mean, twenty-three, Reese? Really? Do they think grownups don't go to the movies?"

He laughed. "Don't ask me. I'm just an actor. I recite the lines and collect my paycheck. I have no clue why they make the marketing choices they do."

"Playing dumb?"

"I'm good at it," he said.

"No. You really aren't."

"Thanks. I'd rather hang out with you than listen to another lecture on box office receipts, too."

She laughed. "So where's the brain trust you came with?"

"She doesn't need me anymore. I got her in the door. Now she's hunting for a steppingstone to the next level."

"Who's she targeting now?"

He chuckled. "She just tried to seduce Sam and it didn't quite pay off. She ended up spilling wine on her dress and went to wash up."

Sam was a director well-known for his innovative indie films. He was also openly gay and would not have been impressed with Felicia's routine.

"I wish I had seen it," Maggie said wryly.

"Yeah. It was something."

"Don't you get tired of all this, Reese?"

"Tired of it?" His expression was deadpan. "Some magazine just named me the sexiest man on the planet. How could I possibly be tired of all this?"

He bent down and ran a hand through the pool water. Then stood back up and shook his hand to dry it. "When I was wasted out of my skull, I would have just dived in."

"Tuxedo and all?" she asked.

"Tuxedo and all." He paused, then said, "listen, about Felicia. I'm really sorry I invited her."

"No problem."

"Yes, she is a problem. She was very rude to you and I feel responsible. I met her at another party last week, and well, she just sort of talked me into bringing her along. And now she made a big scene and interrupted your party."

"Probably livened up the joint," Maggie said with a shrug. "I really don't care, Reese. But she doesn't really seem like your type, to be honest."

He smiled faintly. "I think it was Mick Jagger

who said, *I don't get the women I want; I get the women who want me."*

"And she wanted you," Maggie said.

He shook his head. "She wanted to come to this party. I'm incidental. She's ambitious, and so far, her career is not exactly setting the world on fire."

"So you're the match."

"Yeah. I'm the match to get her little flame going."

"You don't mind being used like that?"

He shrugged. "It's better than being alone. And isn't everybody using everybody else, anyway?" He caught a glimpse of her unguarded expression. "Okay. Not everybody. But it feels like that sometimes, doesn't it?"

She didn't want to tell him she'd been thinking the same thing earlier, so she just shrugged. "How about a cup of coffee? Unless you'd prefer strychnine."

"Coffee would be wonderful."

INSIDE, MAGGIE LED REESE THROUGH THE LIVING room toward Casablanca's front door.

At the entry, the housekeeper was letting in an

already inebriated cinematographer who came lurching toward them, Jack Daniels bottle in hand.

"That's the last thing I need tonight," Reese muttered.

"This way," Maggie said.

They ducked in a side door and shut it behind them.

They were in a wide hallway that led to the guest suite and utility rooms.

"The kitchen's full of catering staff," she explained. "But there's a morning bar in the hall here where we can make coffee in peace."

She quickly found the French press and he rummaged for the coffee, and soon there was water heating in the microwave.

She was just starting to get out the mugs when Reese said, "Do you hear that noise?"

She heard it, too. A scraping sound, like someone was dragging heavy furniture across the oak floor.

They followed the sound down the long hall, past the laundry room and wine cellar.

A cute girl of about nineteen, one of the temporary help, was picking up towels in a guest bath when they passed. "Did you hear that scraping?" Maggie asked her.

"Yeah," the girl said. She was a study in black and

white, dressed in the same uniform all the temp workers wore: white shirt, black polyester pants, and clunky black shoes. She had glossy black hair to her shoulders, and her dark eyes were wide behind black-framed glasses that matched her hair color. The only interruption in the black-and-white theme were her cheeks, which were rosy with exertion.

"Are you okay?" Maggie blurted out, then remembered Mac's *déclassé* comment.

"Yeah," the girl said. "It's just kinda creepy working all alone here with that weird noise. It's been going on for a while. I don't know what it is but I wish it would stop."

"Don't worry," she said. "We'll check it out."

She and Reese continued on until they reached the guest suite at the end of the hall.

"Oh," Maggie said, realizing what the monster behind the closed door was. "The poor thing."

She opened the door and surveyed the destruction inside.

All the furniture had been herded into the center of the room, except for the bed, which was too big for even an eighty-pound dog to move.

But a side table, a small chair, a footstool, and an Aubusson rug that was now ragged at one edge were all piled in the center of the room like a postmodern artwork.

And sitting up on the chair, white paws together, long mane ruffled by the ocean breeze flowing through the open window, head tilted to one side, and sporting a wide, open-mouthed grin, was the most beautiful dog in the world.

"Wow!" Reese said. He went straight to the dog.

The Sable and White Rough Collie, the spitting image of Lassie, gazed adoringly at the people who had come to rescue him from his boredom.

The dog jumped down from his art installation and began rubbing himself on Reese.

"What's his name?" Reese asked.

"Jasper McJasper," she said sarcastically, unable to avoid the scorn that crept into her voice.

"You're kidding."

"Nope."

The dog had shown up at Mac's studio out of the blue just a few weeks ago, and Mac had shipped him up here to Carita to get him out of the way.

The animal had been a token of appreciation for her husband, who had waxed rhapsodic about a country childhood on the farm with his pet Collie while pitching a Christmas movie to shareholders.

He neglected to mention that his childhood farm

had been a New York City brownstone, and that his country life had been spent at a boarding school upstate, and that he'd never even owned a pet hamster, much less a big, rambunctious dog.

So when the movie deal had been signed, the investors had thanked him with the gift of a pedigreed Rough Collie just like the childhood companion he'd tearfully described.

So now Jasper, who Mac McJasper had egotistically named after himself, followed around at his heels whenever he came to Carita. The housekeeper took care of the beast, giving him long runs on the beach and making sure the groomers properly maintained his magnificent coat. And the dog sat and waited for its new owner to have some time for it.

She told the story to Reese, whose frown made clear he understood what she wasn't saying, about Mac's indifference, his lack of interest in anything that wasn't furthering his own ambitions.

"He's not cruel of course," she hastened to add. He just ignored the dog's pleas for attention, treating it much like—

Like he did her. Like he'd gotten a shiny new toy that had been fun for a little while, but now was a dull obligation to be managed by his staff while he went about his business of being rich and important.

Jasper wagged his tail tentatively at her.

"Yeah," she said to the dog. "I know the feeling, you good boy."

Jasper's tail wag grew more enthusiastic at the simple words of praise, and she watched the thick sable brush of it sweep across the side table, taking glossy magazines, coffee table books, and—

"Not that!"

The crystal candy dish hit the oak floor with a dull thud.

Maggie bent to pick it up. The heavy crystal was undamaged, but the wood floor showed a substantial dent.

She'd have to get that fixed before Mac saw it. He was particular about his homes, and wouldn't accept anything less than the best.

"Enough of that, boy," Reese said. He got down on his knees on the floor and played with the dog, who responded with unbridled joy at the attention.

Reese laughed—for real now, not the stage laugh actors used to express polite interest in so many official duties. He was like a boy, rolling on the floor and wrestling with the dog.

The two of them looked like perfection, and she

realized she fit the scene, too, in her glittering custom evening gown.

This would make a great magazine spread, with the stunningly beautiful golden blond man, the picture-perfect dog, and her silvery gown and diamonds, all staged against the backdrop of this pretty, over-decorated room.

She stopped herself. What had happened to her? When had she become unable to just relax and enjoy a moment without seeing the superficial veneer?

When had the fairy tale become all about image and impressing others?

When had she become Maggie McJasper, Hollywood Wife?

Reese was sitting on the floor and staring up at her. The dog panted happily at his side.

"What are you thinking about?" Reese asked her.

"That something went wrong somewhere," she said.

He got it right away. He always did, which was something she'd always enjoyed about talking to him. "This is the life we signed up for," he said. He put his arm around the dog and gazed out the window at the sweep of moonlit sky. "We're stuck with it."

"Maybe," she said.

Reese stood up, brushing off his tuxedo. "You got a plan, Maggie?"

"You're covered in hair," she pointed out.

He shrugged. "I'm Reese Stevens. Nobody will care. So what's the plan?"

She was tired of being an accessory. Tired of being all image and no substance. She turned to Reese. "I have no idea what my plan is."

"Let's start with coffee," he said.

THEY WENT BACK DOWN THE HALL TO THE MORNING bar, the big dog following along. The bathroom was now clean and empty, and the washer in the laundry room was rumbling away.

The girl who had been cleaning was heading out the door to the exit, book bag in hand. She froze when they came near, like a felon caught in the act of escaping the scene of the crime.

She didn't glance their way, but stood, one hand on the doorknob, the other clutching her book bag. She was hunched over as if she expected a knife between her shoulder blades.

"What's going on?" Maggie asked.

"Nothing," she said, but then Felicia pushed the

door open and burst in, the housekeeper Mrs. Queen at her heel.

Abby started to head back down the hall toward the guest suite.

Felicia pointed at the girl. "She's probably got them in there!"

"Come back here, young lady," Mrs. Queen said firmly.

The girl turned around slowly and came back.

"What's going on?" Reese asked Felicia.

"That girl stole my earrings!"

"What?" Maggie noticed Felicia wasn't wearing the beautiful Miyamotos anymore. Even her little diamond ring was gone. "How did she get them away from you?"

Felicia's face was red with anger, making her a little less pretty than before. "They're in there." She pointed at the girl's bag. "I've gotta get those earrings back. I can't afford to lose them."

"But how did this girl take them? What's your name?" Maggie asked the girl.

"Abby Xiong," she said. "And I didn't steal any stupid earrings. I just cleaned the bathroom like I was told to." She glared at Felicia. "She made a big mess and it took me a long time to clean it all up. And then she came back and started yelling at me.

So I just decided to leave...." She trailed off. "I didn't do anything wrong."

"I took my jewelry off to wash up after I spilled wine on myself," Felicia said. "And then when I realized I'd forgotten my stuff and went back to the bathroom, this girl was running away with my jewelry."

"I didn't steal your stuff. I didn't." The girl's voice quaked with fear.

"All right," Maggie said. "Let's all settle down and talk about this. You sit here," she said to Abby, motioning for her to take a stool at the bar. "Why were you running out the door like that?"

"Because she called me a thief. Who's going to listen to me with all these rich people around?"

"Okay. May I take a peek in your bag?"

"No." The girl got a stubborn set to her jaw. "I've got rights."

They heard the doorbell ring again.

"Who could that be?" Maggie asked. "I thought all the guests were here now."

Mrs. Queen went to answer it. She came back with a big graying man who looked one part annoyed and two parts grim.

He held out his identification and Maggie

checked it over. "What can we do for you, Lieutenant Ibarra?"

"You called to report some missing jewelry."

They all turned to Felicia.

"Yes. I called," she said. "I told you, I need those earrings back and the girl was running away with them. Once she's gone I'll never see them again."

"I didn't do it!" Abby shouted. "Stop accusing me!"

Jasper moved in front of Maggie, protecting her from the yelling. She patted his long snout.

"Who else could have done it?" Felicia turned to Lieutenant Ibarra. "I want my earrings back. I don't care about her going to jail, but you've just got to get them back."

"Don't you call me a thief!" Abby yelled.

Jasper let out an ear-piercing bark to add to the shouting.

"Oh, my!" Mrs. Queen said. "That bark would carry over ten miles of heather!"

"Hush!" Maggie said to the dog, who looked crestfallen at being singled out for scolding.

"All right," Ibarra said calmly. "First, I want everyone to shut up."

"Yes," Maggie said. She gave a quick glance toward the open door that led to the entry. The party could be heard out in the living room, and luckily was loud enough to keep anyone from noticing the chaos in the hall.

She nodded her head, and Mrs. Queen shut the door and turned the latch to lock it. "That'll give us a bit o' peace from the hoity-toity."

Maggie patted Jasper's ruff, and he leaned against her hip, almost knocking her over. He grinned to let her know he forgave her for yelling at him.

Lieutenant Ibarra pulled the two bar stools away from the bar. He put one stool against one wall, and the other against the opposite wall. Then he motioned to the two women.

"Both of you just sit down and be quiet."

Abby sat. Felicia sat. The dog sat. On Maggie's instep.

She stifled a yelp and gently removed her Manolo-clad foot from under his belly.

The lieutenant took out a notebook and opened it to a fresh page. He went to stand in front of Felicia. "Now," he said. "Start from the beginning."

In a slightly calmer way, Felicia told the same story she'd shouted at Maggie and Reese before. She took off her jewelry when washing up, and then left Abby to clean the bathroom. When she returned, the jewelry was gone.

He went over to Abby and asked her the same

thing. She said she'd just cleaned up and had no idea what had happened to the jewelry. She'd gone back and forth from the bath to the laundry several times, but passed no one in the hall.

"Do you mind if I check your bag?" he asked Abby.

She clutched it protectively to her chest.

He glanced at the others.

"Okay," Felicia said. "If you need to check." She handed him her small evening bag.

He gave it a quick search. "Thank you," he said, handing it back to her.

Mrs. Queen opened her wool sweater, showing the flowered shirt beneath. "You want to pat me down, young man, you go right ahead," she said briskly. "I don't carry a purse when I'm working."

His gaze briefly touched Reese and Maggie. "I think we can eliminate you two as suspects."

Reese opened his tuxedo jacket and turned his pockets inside out. "It's only fair to check us all."

Maggie turned around in her clingy gown. "I don't have anywhere to hide anything, I'm afraid."

The lieutenant shuffled his feet like he was uncomfortable, then he just gave a curt nod, dismissing them. "I know you people aren't suspects."

"Why?" Abby said. "Because they're rich?"

"Yes, Miss," he said. "Because they're rich. They could buy that jewelry a hundred times over."

"And they weren't around," Mrs. Queen said. "Only you were in this hall, little miss."

"That's not true," Maggie said. "We've been in here making coffee, and we went down the hall to check on the dog."

The cop perked up at that. "Did you see anyone else when you were here?"

Maggie hesitated. "Um…, only Ms. Xiong."

They all stared at the girl.

"I'm sorry," Maggie said to her. "It doesn't mean she did it," she pointed out. "It just means no one saw who might have done it."

"I was by this door the whole time, Mrs. McJasper," Mrs. Queen said. "No one could have gotten past me."

"You took my coat when we arrived and hung it up in that closet across the entry," Reese said. "Have you been doing that all evening?"

"Of course," she said. "But that don't take no more than a minute each time."

"That's fine, ma'am," Ibarra said. He turned to Abby. "All right, young lady. Do you want to sit here while I wake up the judge to get a search warrant for that bag?"

Abby reluctantly handed over her pack and the lieutenant spilled the contents on the bar counter: a physics textbook, wallet, hairbrush, set of keys, and a notebook that fell open to a page with numbers written on it.

At first Maggie assumed the numbers were schoolwork, but then saw they were income and expenses, with frantic scribbling as Abby had tried to work out how to make up a $500 shortfall in tuition payment.

The notebook lay open on the counter like an indictment. They all stared at it.

"I didn't steal anything," the girl said. "I didn't."

"But the earrings have to be in there," Felicia said. "They have to be!"

"Maybe they're just lost," Abby said.

"Lost where? I left them in the bathroom." Felicia's hands were actually trembling. "I can't lose them. They're worth a fortune."

"All right," Ibarra said. "I will get someone out here to check for fingerprints in the bathroom. In the meantime—"

"There aren't any fingerprints in the bathroom," Mrs. Queen said.

"Ma'am?"

"I said, you will not find a fingerprint in that

bathroom. I always follow up on temporary workers, and that bathroom is clean."

"But, Ma'am, there still could be—"

"I said I cleaned that bathroom," Mrs. Queen said. "That means it is clean. There will not be a fingerprint in that room."

"Maybe you missed a spot."

Maggie shook her head at the detective. "Um, Lieutenant, I wouldn't...."

Mrs. Queen drew herself up to her full five-foot-two height, cloaked in the disgust of a twenty-year veteran of the housekeeping wars. "I. Don't. Miss. Spots." The temperature in the room dropped by ten degrees at her tone.

"Fine," he said. "And no one else was in this part of the house except Ms. Dalton, Ms. Xiong, Ms. Queen—"

"—*Missus* Queen." Her voice was still icy as the tundra.

"Mrs. Queen," he corrected himself, "and Mrs. McJasper and Mr. Stevens."

"Not that we know of," Maggie said. "But maybe —" She stopped herself. She hated to even suggest another of the locals could be involved. "Give me a minute," she said to the cop.

She quickly found the caterer and asked him a

question, then came back into the hall, thinking furiously.

"The caterer had all his staff in his sight in the main room and kitchen for the last hour," she reported to Lieutenant Ibarra. "Nobody's unaccounted for."

"Except for Ms. Xiong," he said.

Maggie nodded reluctantly.

"And how about the others?"

She knew what *others* he meant. The only others who were in the house this evening were the carefully curated guest list of big shots. She pursed her lips, knowing Big Mac would throw a fit if she even suggested a party guest could be a thief.

"Maybe there isn't a thief at all," Abby said desperately. "Maybe the earrings are just lost. Maybe they're just stuck in the towels. I left them in the laundry basket."

"I put them towels in the wash," Mrs. Queen said. "I shook them out. There was nothing in them towels."

"Maybe you missed—" Lieutenant Ibarra began, but stopped when Mrs. Queen shot him a glare. "Okay, so you didn't miss them."

He tapped his notebook with one finger and gave Maggie a sideways glance, and carefully broached the unasked question. "I don't suppose you'd let me talk to the guests about this?"

He said it with just the tiniest query in his voice. Clearly Lieutenant Ibarra knew how Carita worked.

The big shots on The Row would not react kindly if he interrupted their party to interrogate them.

Maggie knew how unfair it was, but she couldn't quite bring herself to face the consequences of telling him, *Sure. Question this group of very rich, spoiled, fussy people. It's not like you wanted to keep your pension or anything.*

Ibarra closed the notebook with a snap and put it in his pocket. "Then we're done here. I need you two young women to come downtown with me."

"But you can't charge her based on this," Maggie protested. "This isn't evidence."

"I'm not charging her. I am taking her in for questioning. You too," Ibarra said to Felicia. "I'll need you to sign a statement."

"Fine," Felicia said. "But where are my earrings?"

"I have no idea," he said. "But she'll tell us."

Abby sobbed. "My parents will die of shame."

"Is this really necessary?" Reese asked.

"Well, *Sir,* since I am not allowed to question the guests, and I've been notified that there aren't any fingerprints at the alleged crime scene, yes, I would say the next step is to get official statements from the two parties involved."

Ibarra saw Maggie about to protest, and he said, "Ma'am, I'm not enjoying this any more than you are. I was looking forward to a bowl of chili and the late-late show. But a complaint has been made, and I have to investigate." He frowned. "As much as I am allowed to."

"Chili?" Maggie said thoughtfully.

"Yes. Chili. It's what those of us who aren't rich eat sometimes."

"I know. My dad's Chile Verde is to die for. But I was just thinking...."

"Yes?"

"Mrs. Queen, I don't suppose there's much of that prime rib left, is there?"

"Oh, I believe there's a goodly amount still out there," she said. "They've probably finished packing away the charcuterie, but the big dinner display is all there."

"Prime rib?" Lieutenant Ibarra asked.

"Prime rib," Maggie said. "With fingerling baked potatoes," she added. "Stuffed with brie and bacon."

The lieutenant gazed down his ample nose at her.

"Are you suggesting I can be bribed with prime rib, Mrs. McJasper?"

"Of course not. But I *am* suggesting that you should probably eat a little something to tide you over until you can get home."

"Because you're so concerned about my growling stomach?" he asked with a raised eyebrow.

"Because it would give me time to talk to the guests, and to check out the laundry, and to see if the earrings fell into a floor vent, and—"

"Exactly how long do you think it's going to take for me to eat a little piece of prime rib?"

"With baked potatoes," Reese said. "Stuffed with brie and bacon."

"And chocolate cake for dessert," Maggie added.

"One hour," Lieutenant Ibarra said. "It will take me one hour. No more."

WITHOUT A WORD, MRS. QUEEN HAD GOTTEN A LINT roller out of a drawer, and turned Reese around to remove every bit of dog hair from his tuxedo.

"That's good enough, Ma'am," he had said while she fussed over his suit. "You can stop."

"I don't miss spots," she said, giving his once-again immaculate tuxedo an approving nod.

"Thank you, Ma'am," he said very seriously, barely stifling a grin.

"Now," Mrs. Queen said, turning to Maggie, "I'll check the bathroom again, just to make sure."

"No," Maggie said. "I will search, and talk to people, and all that."

"What should I do?" she asked.

"You keep those two women on those stools in opposite corners."

Jasper leaned against her leg, pushing her up against the wall.

"And you keep the dog here out of the way."

"Anything else?" she asked.

"Yes," Maggie said. "You keep that man's plate full while I try to figure out what happened."

REESE FOLLOWED HER DOWN THE HALL. "SO WHAT DO we do first?" he asked.

"We?"

"Yeah. We. This is way more interesting than the party. You're not going to leave me out of your investigation. So where do we start?"

"I figured I'd retrace Felicia's steps," Maggie said. "She took the earrings off in the bathroom. We'll start there. See if they fell down a vent or under a cabinet or something. Then I'll check the laundry room. Then check the laundry itself."

"You're assuming they just fell into a crack somewhere," he said.

"I'm not assuming anything. I'm trying to figure out what happened without jumping to conclusions like Lieutenant Ibarra."

They headed down the hall, looking along the baseboards for any telltale glimmer of diamonds.

"I don't believe her," she said.

"You just said you weren't jumping to conclusions," Reese said. "Now you sound just like the cop."

"No," she corrected. "I wasn't talking about Abby. I'm trying to figure out if I automatically disbelieve Felicia because she's an entitled little brat, or if I think she's lying."

"Oh. Well, I'm with you there. I don't believe a word she says either."

"She's your girlfriend," Maggie pointed out.

"Date. Not girlfriend. We don't even like each other."

"Why do you hang out with someone who doesn't like you?"

"Well who *does* like me?" he asked.

"I do."

He smiled that devastating smile. "Wow. That means something."

"Charmer," she said sarcastically.

"No." He stopped smiling. "It means something. You aren't a phony like most of these people. I like you, too. And not in a getting-in-your-pants kind of way, either."

His gaze roved over her glimmering gown. "Though I'd like you that way, too, if you weren't married."

She laughed. "You are absolutely incorrigible."

He sighed. "I like literacy, too."

"Literacy?"

"You use words like incorrigible. I miss the lost art of intelligent conversation."

They reached the bathroom. He gestured her inside. "We'd better get this search done quickly, before they start a rumor about us."

"They won't start a rumor about us," she said. "I'm old enough to be your—"

"—equal?"

"Yeah." She laughed. "But about Felicia. I think

she's a conniving little—" She stopped. "You know. But I do believe she's genuinely worried about losing those earrings."

"She's not a good enough actress to act that scared if she's not really upset," he agreed.

"Of course you actors are good at faking sincerity."

"The key thing to being an actor is honesty," he said. "Once you can fake that, you've got it made."

She laughed.

"I can't remember who said it, but this party is living proof."

"If you hate Mac's parties, why did you come?"

"Because I couldn't picture spending this particular night alone at home, staring at the walls."

"Yeah," she agreed. "People like to get all dressed up and party on New Year's Eve."

"New Year's Eve. Right," he said softly. Then he clapped his hands together. "So what do we do first?"

MAGGIE LET REESE GET DOWN ON HIS KNEES AND check all the spots in the bathroom where the jewelry might have fallen.

"Nothing," he said, after feeling around under the

cabinet, and even putting his hand behind the toilet to check if the earrings had rolled back there.

"Ugh," Maggie said. "You don't have to go quite that far."

He stood up and brushed off the knees of his tuxedo trousers, which didn't show the tiniest speck of dirt from his exploits, proving Mrs. Queen's point about her housekeeping abilities. "Why not? Do you think the old biddy was lying about the room being all spit-and-polished?"

"No," she said. "A speck o' dirt wouldn't dare land here while she's on duty."

Maggie stood there in the spacious guest bath, her arms crossed in front of her and tapping her elbows with her fingertips. She stared at the silver fish pattern on the custom wallpaper. The koi stared back, mocking her.

"Maybe they'll just charge the girl with a misdemeanor," Reese said hopefully. "This might not be such a big deal."

"It is a big deal. Those Miyamotos are worth about a quarter-million dollars," she said. "And Mac is going to kill me if this whole thing ends up in the press."

"Not really," Reese said.

"Of course not really," she replied. "But he'll be

disappointed in me for not managing the problem and for allowing it to turn into a scandal."

"Too bad, because the earrings are definitely not in this room," he said.

She sighed. "I miss the good old days."

Reese leaned against the bathroom counter. "The what?"

"You know. Haven't you read any Agatha Christie novels?"

"I've always been more of a Raymond Chandler type, actually," he said.

"That figures. But in all the old mysteries, the detective would search the room where the crime took place and there'd always be a monogrammed handkerchief or an engraved silver compact with the initials HB, and he'd immediately know that Hildegard von Bingen was the dastardly killer."

"Yeah," he said. "Monograms have gone out of style. Also, people maybe aren't that stupid."

"I'm just saying, we've got nothing. A good monogrammed hanky would be helpful right about now."

Reese smiled. "Let's assume for the moment that old Hildegard didn't do it. It's got to be someone at the party. So let's line them all up and search them."

"Yeah," Maggie said. "And we would be pariahs in Hollywood forever."

"You say that like it's a bad thing," Reese said with a raised eyebrow.

"Mac would kill me," she said. "We can do that as a last resort. But for now, let's keep this under wraps so I don't have to sleep in the guest room with the dog tonight. If the thief is smart, they'll have hidden the jewels where no one would stumble across them."

"So let's do some stumbling," he said. "We can search all the places they could be hidden. I've got nothing better to do. Have you?"

"Nope. I don't have any better idea, anyway."

Reese motioned to the doorway. "Let's leave Saint Hildegard in peace and try the laundry room."

THEY TOOK TURNS PULLING WET TOWELS OUT OF THE washer and going over them, inch by inch, looking for any jewelry that might have gotten snagged in the fabric.

"How are you so sure the earrings are worth that much money?" Reese asked.

"Jewelry is my hobby," she said.

"Good thing you married rich," he said.

"Not this kind of jewelry." She motioned to her diamond earrings. "I mean, Mac's given me a lot of pretty things over the last ten years. But I'm more into beadwork, creating designs out of crystals and beadweaving and things like that. Not real jewelry. It's too boring."

"Boring?"

"Yeah. Anybody with money can buy incredible earrings. But if you create a design yourself out of beads, it's more interesting."

"Big Mac must be thrilled to save all that money."

"He forbids me to wear my boho designs in public. Says it's not fitting for someone married to him to wear cheap stuff."

Reese opened his mouth to say something, then shut it again. He focused on the towel he was holding for a minute, then changed the subject by saying, "means, motive, and opportunity."

She glanced at him. "I guess you really did read those Chandler books."

He shook his head. "I played a cop in a *Law & Order: SVU* episode. I spouted stuff like that."

"I remember. Your big comeback. You won an Emmy."

"Yeah," he grimaced. "They love to give awards for autobiographical parts like that."

"Autobiography? You played a cop."

"I played a junkie."

"Right," she said quietly. "So how close are you to the EGOT?" The EGOT was the ultimate awards grand slam: Emmy, Grammy, Oscar, Tony.

He shrugged. "I'll never get that. I'll forever be just an EG." He pronounced it *egg*.

"You've got time. Why not go for it?"

He shook his head. "Big Mac talked me into playing king of the vampires in that reboot. I don't think the Academy is going to be impressed by the fangs."

She laughed. "I suppose not."

He dropped the last towel into the dryer. "Nothing here. So let's see: our thief needed to have opportunity. That points back to the girl. She was the only one in the bathroom."

"But I just realized something," Maggie said. "Mrs. Queen thought nobody could have gone past her without being seen. But she didn't see us come into the hall because she was busy answering the door. If she got that detail wrong, maybe she missed other people wandering around where they shouldn't be."

"Or maybe she's lying," Reese pointed out. "What if she took the jewelry?"

"Mrs. Queen? Of course not."

"Why not? The butler always did it."

"We don't have a butler."

"Exactly. You have the perfect suspect: the housekeeper. A sweet round Irish lady who no one would ever suspect. We missed these." He leaned over the washer and pulled out one more towel and a washcloth. He handed the washcloth to Maggie, and continued, "If we accuse Mrs. Queen, she'll probably say, *faith and begorra, I never heard o' such a thing!*"

He added the last in an exaggerated brogue.

"You're right," Maggie said. "Don't hold your breath waiting for that Oscar."

He laughed. "So what about the housekeeper? Why should we assume she's forgetful and not nefarious?"

"She's not a movie character, Reese. Mrs. Queen has worked for Mac for about twenty years."

"Maybe she has a hot young boyfriend. He stole the jewels and she's covering up for him."

"Mrs. Queen is a widow with a teenage son. Her husband owned the barber shop in downtown Carita."

"You mean the hole-in-the-wall on the main drag with the big barber pole out front? I was going to stop in and say hello while I was in town, but it looked empty."

"It is empty. He died months ago. Mr. Queen cut hair for all the old geezers in town. Don't tell me you went to him."

"Of course not. Ramos does my hair. My stylist would have a fit if anyone else touched it. But I remember Mr. Queen. He had no idea who I was, but he was a nice old guy who said hi every time I passed. So maybe his son's a crook."

"You are so cynical. Patrick is at a party with his friends."

Reese threw his last towel into the dryer. "Nothing here. So where do you think the girl hid the jewelry?"

"No," Maggie said firmly. "I just don't think it is Abby."

"Why?"

She stopped there, holding the final wet towel at arms' length so it wouldn't drip on her dress. She pondered the question for a bit. "I don't know why. Maybe it's me. Maybe I just remember being her. Working my way through college. Maybe that's affecting my judgment. Maybe it is as simple as it appears: broke student steals to cover her tuition."

"Or maybe not," he said.

"Who else could it be?"

"I don't know. But there's a whole roomful of suspects we haven't questioned yet."

Maggie put the towel into the dryer and hit the start button. "Then let's start grilling them."

MAGGIE MINGLED FOR A WHILE, SOMEHOW ALWAYS bringing the subject around to where everyone had been in the last hour.

Reese did the same, and after they'd covered pretty much everyone at the party, they met up again.

"Nothing," she said.

"Nothing for me, either," Reese said. "No one saw anyone go into that hallway. Let's face it: these people wouldn't leave this room if the building was on fire. They all want to be where the action is."

"I don't know what—" Maggie started to say, but Reese interrupted with a jolly, "Sam!"

Sam, the director who'd been the victim of

Felicia's attempted lovebombing earlier, gave Reese a big hug.

"How've you been?" Reese asked with what appeared to be genuine interest.

Sam seemed flattered, even blushing a little. "Fine, fine."

They chatted about their latest projects for a bit, and then Reese said, "sorry about Felicia."

"Not a problem," Sam said. "She's not exactly your type, I would've thought."

Maggie lifted her hands in the air. "That's what I said to him."

"So why'd you pick her?" Sam asked.

"She picked me. They usually do."

"You could have said no," Sam pointed out.

Reese shrugged. "Have you seen her legs?"

"I didn't notice," Sam replied with a bemused smile. "But then that's why I'm not a fashion photographer." He smiled at Maggie. "As far as I'm concerned, she can go right back to Hong Kong or Timbuktu or wherever she's been modeling. I don't mean to be sexist, but there are some women who should be seen and not heard."

"Some men, too," Maggie said dryly.

"Fair enough."

Reese shook Sam's hand and said, "well, I think

I'll buy our hostess a drink. See you later."

He took Maggie by the arm and steered her in the direction of the bar. "I don't think he did it," he said. "He's disgusted with her, but doesn't seem petty enough to steal her jewelry." He ran a hand through his hair. "I don't know, Maggie. No one has a motive."

"Sam has a crush on you," Maggie pointed out.

"I know," he said. "He has for years. But he knows that's not going to happen."

"You don't think he could be jealous of Felicia?" she asked. "He sure doesn't like her."

"You don't like her, and you didn't steal her stuff."

They went into an alcove off the main living room. It led to a sweeping stairway. There was a velvet rope across the stairs to keep the partygoers out of the private rooms upstairs.

Reese unhooked the rope and led Maggie up the stairs. "We haven't searched here."

"You said yourself that no one would leave the party for fear of missing out on making connections with someone important," Maggie reminded him.

"I know. But we're running out of options." He sighed as they climbed. "I really hate this. That kid is going to spend the night in jail."

"Do you think she could be convicted on such

slim evidence?" Maggie asked.

He shook his head. "Logically, you wouldn't think so. But I don't trust that cop. He seemed to think he had enough to haul her in just on Felicia's guess about what happened."

"Could we be wrong?" she asked. "Is it possible she's guilty, and is just playing innocent because she got caught?"

"Maybe," he said.

Maggie stood at the top of the stairs and stared out a window at the panoramic view of Carita Cove. "I felt like I was looking in a mirror when I saw her." She frowned. "Maybe that's making me biased. Maybe I'm stupid to believe some teenager just because she reminds me of myself at that age."

"Be stupid," Reese said.

"What?"

"Be idealistic. For once. Let's both believe in something."

"I'll try," she said.

They started searching all the upstairs rooms.

"SHHH!" MAGGIE WARNED. "NOT THAT DOOR. IT'S Mac's office and he's on that important call."

But Reese had already opened the door and peered in. Then he quickly stepped back, pulling the door shut.

He turned and faced her. His expression was totally blank. "Where do we try next?" he asked.

"Why do you look like that?" she asked. "What's in there? A dead body?"

She tried to go around him, but he put his hands on her shoulders. "Don't, Maggie."

She shook him off and opened the door.

Mac was happier than he had been in ages. The woman was curvy, like her. About twenty-five, like Maggie had been when she'd been Big Mac McJasper's secretary and he had told her that his old hag of a wife was mean and vindictive and didn't understand him.

Now it was Maggie's turn to be the mean old hag in the story.

Big Mac's tuxedo would never be the same once his secretary was through with him. Not secretary. Personal assistant. And she was getting very personal.

So personal that neither of them noticed the door open.

Maggie eased the door shut and turned away.

"Maybe I should get a tattoo on my rear like

hers," Maggie muttered.

"Please don't," he said.

"Why not?" Maggie said. "I tried everything else."

"It's time to stop trying," he said bluntly.

"Yes. It's past time to stop trying," Maggie said softly. She sighed. "Her name's Virginia. Obviously not an appropriate name. She works for him at the studio."

"I'll bet she does," Reese said. "I'm sorry."

She threw her shoulders back. "Don't be. I think I knew. I wasn't listening to my gut until now, but I knew."

Those blue eyes of his were too intense. She turned away.

"Are you gonna be okay?"

"Yeah." She thought about it. "Yeah. I think I am. I'm sure later I'll have a good cry, but after that, I think I'll be okay."

"I knew there was some reason I always liked you, Magdalena Lopez."

"I can't believe you remember my maiden name."

"I was at the wedding, remember?"

"Yeah. You went to your boss's wedding ten years ago. But how do you even remember that kind of detail?"

"When I first got sober, everything was crystal

clear for a while. I remember every detail from that time. It was like coming out of a coma."

Maggie sat down on a bench in the hall.

Reese sat down next to her, loosened his bow tie, and unbuttoned the top button on his pleated tuxedo shirt. "I need to breathe," he muttered.

She played with the chipped acrylic nail on her ring finger. It snagged on her shimmering gown and she muttered a curse while she worked to get it loose. The ragged nail clashed with the five carat engagement ring and matching diamond-encircled wedding band she wore.

"I've never liked diamonds," she said, looking at her fingers. "I like pretty colors and fun patterns and things I make with my own two hands. Not jewels and platinum. I told him that, but he kept buying me all this flashy junk."

"I'm sorry, Maggie."

"Mac never even liked my name," she muttered. "Magdalena Lopez, I mean."

"Magdalena? It's a pretty name."

"The Lopez part always bothered him."

"Really?" he said, his voice chilly.

"No. Not what you're thinking. It's because my dad's Lucky Lopez and it bugged Mac to be reminded of that."

"Your dad is Lucky Lopez, the Car King of Cupertino?"

"You've heard of him?"

"Sure. I remember his old TV commercials. But that's nothing to be embarrassed about."

"I'm not embarrassed. My dad is a great guy. He built his business from scratch into one of the top dealerships in the state. But Mac likes people to think I'm... fancy. Like the people here."

"Oh, please. Nobody at this party is fancy. It's all phony. Every bit of it."

"I don't know, Reese." Her gaze roved over the tuxedo-clad movie star from head to toe. "You're pretty fancy."

"No, I'm not. I'm Stanley Tibbets from Deep Creek, California."

"Stanley Tibbets?"

"Yup. Really. I was named after my grandfather."

"I did not know that. I mean, I knew about Deep Creek, of course." *Deep Creek* was the name of the teenage rock band that had burst onto the scene twenty years ago, propelled to fame by a charismatic lead singer who eventually went from fronting a band to acting in hit movies. "Stanley," she said softly.

"Yeah. Nora came up with the name Reese Stevens when she found us."

Nora McJasper was his manager, the woman who had discovered Reese playing at a county fair when he was just a kid.

Nora was also Big Mac's ex-wife, the mean old hag he had told Maggie about when she was young and stupid and believed him.

Maggie had later learned that the first Mrs. McJasper was actually a charming woman who was so nice she was friends with pretty much everyone in Los Angeles.

Even Maggie herself, the woman who had replaced her.

The only reason Nora wasn't at the party tonight was because she was now happily married to a lovely man who worshipped her, and had better things to do on New Year's Eve than kiss up to a bunch of industry hacks. Maggie wondered if her own turn at being the ex-Mrs. McJasper would go as well.

"You okay?" Reese asked.

"Yeah." She sniffed to clear up the tears that were stinging her eyes a bit. "I never would have pegged you for a Stanley." Then she thought of something. "Isn't that the character in *Foul Play*?"

"Never heard of it," he said, his expression blank.

"The movie, *Foul Play,* from back in the 1970s."

"Before your time."

"Of course, nitwit. But it was great. Starred Goldie Hawn."

"Kate Hudson's mother?" He sounded confused.

"Yes, you dope. Goldie Hawn plays a secretary who stumbles into a murder plot, and one of those guys from *Saturday Night Live* plays the handsome cop."

"John Belushi," he said.

"No. You're playing me, aren't you?"

He grinned. "Just a little. *Foul Play*. 1978. Set in San Francisco. Goldie Hawn plays a librarian, not a secretary, and Chevy Chase is a police detective who thinks she's nuts, but falls in love with her anyway. Dudley Moore stole the movie as Stanley Tibbets."

"You know it pretty well."

"Dudley Moore plays a character with my name. Of course I know it."

"Is that why Nora wanted you to change your name?"

"I changed it because Stanley Tibbets didn't fit on the *Tiger Beat* magazine posters. You remember those?"

"Vaguely," she said. His poster had graced the wall

of her bedroom when she was twelve, but she wasn't about to tell him that.

Maggie glanced back down the hall to Big Mac's office. "We'd better move on."

"Can we? I think we're stuck."

"We'll figure it out," she said.

"No, Maggie. I mean we're stuck. We made our choices when we were young and foolish, and now this is the life we've got. I'm dating a woman who would shoot me between the eyes if it would get her a walk-on in the next James Wan picture. And you're married to a man who's too old for you, too dumb for you, and too unfaithful for you."

"Geez, when you put it that way, maybe we should just slit our wrists and be done with it."

He frowned. "Not even as a joke, Maggie."

She glanced at his wrists, still bearing the faint scars. "Sorry, Stanley."

He stood up, then held out his hand to her.

She took it and he lifted her to her feet.

"Enough of the self-pity," he said. "This poor kid is being railroaded."

"And we're running out of options."

Reese headed back to the hall in a last-ditch effort to keep Lieutenant Ibarra at bay, but Maggie spotted Cassidy Carter, an actress at about the same level as Felicia, and decided to see if she could learn anything from her.

Cassidy was canoodling with the droning accountant. He wasn't droning at the moment. He could hardly take a breath with her on him like an octopus. Maggie had to give the woman credit for ambition.

When they came up for air, the man seemed shellshocked.

Cassidy gave him the glitzy smile that had won her several toothpaste commercials, and then sauntered to the bar for a drink.

Maggie made her way over to greet her. Cassidy gave Maggie the smile she reserved for people whose husbands could help her career, and said hello.

After a few pleasantries, Maggie congratulated her on her latest sitcom part (*Beautiful Cashier #3*). Cassidy preened at the praise. Then Maggie casually steered the talk to Felicia.

"I understand Felicia Dalton's career has been really heating up," Maggie dropped into the conversation.

"Oh, please. She's not hot."

"Do you know her?"

"Sure. Known her for years."

"I see. So what's she been up to?"

"She was modeling in Hong Kong last I heard. But with those fake implants of hers I doubt she was getting too much work over there. Then she suddenly waltzes back into town and starts auditioning for commercial spots again. Thinks she's gonna get all the jobs."

"The jobs you want."

"The jobs I deserve. I've put in my time."

"I'm sure you have," Maggie said dryly.

Cassidy got huffy, so Maggie quickly backtracked. "Felicia's not the nicest person I've ever met," she said, maneuvering to see what Cassidy knew about the whole affair.

"She's a jerk," Cassidy said. "There's no give and take with her; she's just out for herself."

"Give and take?"

"She has different diamonds for every day of the week, but she won't even pick up a check for drinks at Chateau Marmont, you know?"

"Really? If her career is on the skids, where does she get so much jewelry?"

"From her boyfriend, of course."

"Her boyfriend?"

"Yeah." Cassidy tossed her hair back and accepted a second white wine spritzer from the local college kid who was tending bar. She thanked him with a dazzling smile. The bartender took a step back as if dizzy.

Cassidy focused her attention on him, but he turned to Maggie. "How's Abby?" he asked.

Maggie shook her head. "Nothing's certain yet."

"*Hello,*" Cassidy said pointedly to the man. How dare someone not make her the center of their attention.

"Sorry," he muttered. "My friend is gonna be arrested for stealing that actress's earrings if they can't find 'em."

"Too bad," Cassidy said indifferently. Then she turned to Maggie. "That's why you're asking about Felicia? She lost her earrings?"

Maggie nodded.

Cassidy laughed out loud. She raised her spritzer and saluted. "Good."

Maggie saw the bartender bristle, so she gestured for him to leave them alone. He walked away, his back stiff with anger.

Cassidy's surprise at Felicia's missing jewelry had seemed genuine, but who could tell with these actors?

Maggie toyed with a drink napkin. It was black linen, emblazoned with a silver BIG MAC logo. She saw her dear husband strolling into the party across the room, his secretary entering a discrete ten feet behind him, still adjusting her skirt.

Mac headed over to Maggie. When he got there, he leaned in for a kiss, but she just happened to turn her head away and his lips brushed her cheek instead.

"Did your call go well?" she asked brightly.

"Fine," he said. "You know—just business as usual."

"Yeah. I know." When he seemed ready to settle in at her side for a while, she nodded to the crowd. "You need to mingle. Everyone's missed you."

He smiled his big smile and headed off to gladhand his guests.

She turned back to Cassidy, who appeared about to leave, disappointed at not meeting the famous producer.

"Oh," Maggie said. "I forgot to introduce you to my husband. I'll do that next time he comes around."

That got Cassidy to happily hang out with her and chat a bit longer.

Maggie kept playing with the napkin and, after a bit more back-and-forth about the party, she innocently asked, "you said Felicia got the fancy jewelry from her boyfriend. Do you mean Reese Stevens?"

"Reese?" She glanced disdainfully at Maggie. "Are you kidding? Reese is for party invitations. The boyfriend's for jewelry."

Isn't everybody using everybody else? Reese had said.

Maggie felt the linen tear in her hands. She saw she'd ripped right across the silver BIG MAC logo. She ran her finger over the rip, knowing it was beyond repair.

"So who was the jewelry guy?" she asked casually. "Someone I know?"

Cassidy finished her spritzer with a gulp and motioned to the bartender, who didn't appear to see her.

"The jewelry guy?" Maggie repeated.

"Daniel Krakower," Cassidy said.

Maggie was acquainted with Daniel Krakower, the owner of Best Jewelers on Rodeo Drive. She remembered him telling her about his daughter's ballet class last time she'd been in there to pick up a bracelet. He was a sweet (but rather homely) little man with a receding hairline and an expanding waistline. "I thought he was married. Dorothy or Donna or something?"

"Duh." Again the disdain, like Maggie was the most naïve little country bumpkin Cassidy had ever run across. "Felicia was milking him like the cash cow he was. He'd let her have anything in the store. But I bet he'll kill her for losing those earrings."

"Yeah," Maggie said. "And that wouldn't bother you at all, would it?"

"Nope," Cassidy said. "I wouldn't shed a tear."

Maggie didn't bother to mention that with a face full of botox, it was unlikely Cassidy could shed a tear if her life depended on it.

So she just said a polite goodbye, dumped the torn napkin in the trash, and went in search of Reese to tell him what she'd learned.

SHE FOUND REESE WITH THE LIEUTENANT.

Abby perched on her stool, her head down and her fingers clenched around her book bag. Felicia sat on her stool, shoulders hunched, miserable.

Mrs. Queen hovered.

The dog circled them all looking worried about the tension in the room.

And Lieutenant Ibarra placidly ate his cake.

Maggie and Reese stood by the door and

compared notes.

"We've got nothing," she moaned. "Nothing at all."

"We've got too many suspects," he agreed, keeping his voice low.

"Yeah. But we don't have a single bit of evidence against any of them." She counted off on her fingers: "Sam is jealous of Felicia, but I can't imagine him doing something so petty."

Reese nodded. "Before we have the police question a BAFTA-nominated director, we'd better have something more than a harmless crush. But I still have my doubts about Mrs. Queen," he added.

"Based on what?"

"She had access," he insisted. "She's as likely a suspect as Abby." He said thoughtfully, "there really isn't anybody else."

"Not true," Maggie said. "Cassidy Carter is thrilled at Felicia's misfortune. But I don't know if she could have gone to the bathroom without being noticed. And I'm not sure she's a good-enough actress to pull off the surprised expression she gave me when I told her about the theft."

"And the same goes for Felicia," he agreed. "She's not a good enough actress to pull off such a huge lie. She's really scared about losing those earrings. So we're out of options."

Lieutenant Ibarra cleared his throat.

"And we're out of time," Maggie said.

They headed back to the group.

Lieutenant Ibarra took the last bite of chocolate cake, wiped his mouth with a napkin, and set his plate in the sink.

"Can't we get this over with?" Felicia said. "I'm gonna have to find a way to explain this to...." She trailed off.

"To your boyfriend?" Maggie said.

"Yeah," Felicia said. "And he's gonna kill me if I don't have those earrings."

"Is the boyfriend insured?" Ibarra asked Felicia.

"I don't know. What if he isn't?"

"Then we need to find where this girl hid the jewels. If he's insured, he can collect the insurance. If not, maybe he'll kill you."

"And maybe he won't kill you," Maggie said. "Though his wife might."

"We've looked everywhere," Maggie said to Abby. "I'm really sorry."

"Thank you for trying," she said. "I don't know what I'm going to do. I could get expelled. My parents are going to be so upset."

"We still haven't searched the guests," Reese pointed out.

"I don't think we can get away with strip-searching the most powerful people in Hollywood," Maggie said.

"Some of them might like it," Reese said absently.

"You're right about that. But if we even suggest it, every person in there is going to speed-dial their lawyer and we'll never hear the end of it."

Lieutenant Ibarra came over to Abby. "Stand up. It's time to go."

Maggie whispered to herself, "Hong Kong."

Reese turned to her. "Yes?"

She motioned to him.

He bent down and she whispered something in his ear.

She then put one hand gently on Lieutenant Ibarra's arm. "Give us one more minute?"

He raised an eyebrow, but waited.

Reese went over to Felicia. She gazed up at him warily, but he just took her in his arms and leaned down as if to kiss her. She smiled and closed her eyes and lifted her face to his.

He ran his hands seductively over her body, and then stopped at her bra.

"Do I rip it off you, or do you hand them over?" he said, his voice icy.

She reached into her neckline and pulled out the

earrings and ring.

Mrs. Queen gasped, Abby burst into tears, and Lieutenant Ibarra slapped his hand on the granite counter so hard the dog jumped.

Reese handed the pieces to Maggie. "Is this the missing jewelry?"

Jasper came back to hug close against Maggie's side again. She gave him a quick pat on the head, then ignored him and examined the jewelry.

Up close, Maggie saw that the ring was just a simple half-carat solitaire, the kind you could get in any mall.

"Your birthday is in April?" she asked, and Felicia nodded.

"Why?" Detective Ibarra asked.

"Because diamond is the April birthstone, and little rings like this one, with a white sapphire, make an affordable birthstone ring, since most people can't afford real diamonds." She glanced up at Felicia. "This ring is yours, isn't it?"

She nodded. "It's my stuff."

"That's not exactly what I meant," Maggie muttered. She handed the ring to Felicia, who put it on her finger.

But when Felicia held out her hand for the earrings, Maggie said, "Not so fast."

She held up one of the earrings. It glittered in the halogen spotlight that illuminated the breakfast bar.

"Wow," Lieutenant Ibarra said. "Those are really something. So you think it was insurance fraud?"

Maggie held the other earring up to the light, examining the brilliance of the diamonds.

Then she laughed. "I was right." Then she glanced at Ibarra. "No, it's not insurance fraud."

Reese stared coldly at Felicia. "I figured you must be telling the truth because you weren't that good of an actress. I guess you're better than I thought."

"No," Maggie said. "She isn't that good. She just found the kernel of truth in her character and played it to the hilt."

"What are you talking about?" Lieutenant Ibarra said. He stood in front of Felicia. "Explain yourself."

Felicia crossed her arms over her ample chest and glared at Maggie. "You think you're so smart. You explain."

"Okay," Maggie said. "It had nothing to do with Abby. Nothing to do with the party, or anyone here. This was all a last-ditch effort to save herself from Daniel Krakower."

"Daniel Krakower?" Reese said. "That little guy? I've known his family for years. He wouldn't hurt a fly."

"He might, if she borrowed earrings he couldn't afford to lose and refused to return them."

"I still don't get it," the lieutenant said.

"I'll explain," Maggie said. "Felicia Dalton was messing around with a married man, a jeweler named Daniel Krakower. She wore different diamond earrings every time Cassidy Carter saw her. There is no way he would give her a different valuable pair like this every day. He must have been letting her *borrow* jewelry in exchange for... whatever she exchanged for the privilege. Then she got a modeling job in Hong Kong and left for several months, taking some of the borrowed pieces with her."

"That's right," Reese said. "Sam said she'd been modeling in Hong Kong."

"So did Cassidy," Maggie said. "But she said Felicia wasn't succeeding at it and headed home after losing some jobs. So she came back to town, thinking she could just waltz back into her old life: getting commercial and modeling work, and using Krakower for her fancy jewelry habit. But something had changed. The spell was broken with Krakower. Maybe his wife got suspicious. Maybe he just got tired of her."

"That could happen," Reese said dryly.

"Yeah. So suddenly she's in a bind. He wants the borrowed stuff back. So she has to scramble and find a way to explain why she can't return the pieces to him."

"You lost me," Lieutenant Ibarra said. "They're right there." He pointed to the earrings Maggie was holding.

She turned back to Felicia. "I mean, the pearls are really nice. Majorca, right? But the cubic zirconia is just too perfect."

"Too perfect?" the lieutenant asked.

"Yes. Real diamonds have a color tinge to them. You can actually see a rainbow in them in the right light. And they have flaws—little inclusions and features that give them the unique charm of a real stone. A cubic zirconia is cold white, clear as glass, and assembly-line perfect."

"Are you sure?"

"Oh, yeah," she said. "I'm sure. And more importantly, any jeweler would be. And there's more. The white gold plating must be very thin—one of the settings is chipped and the base metal is showing through."

She glanced over at Felicia's very red face. "I think you got a bit ripped off there."

"They're fakes," the lieutenant said.

"Good fakes. But these aren't Miyamotos. They aren't the quality of the real thing. Oh, sure, if you see them from a distance, they look beautiful. But if you know pearls, if you know diamonds, and if you know the little details of jewelry, it's clear these are counterfeit."

"You're not suggesting Krakower sells fakes?" Ibarra asked.

"Of course not. He's a reputable jeweler. But I am saying some of the best jewelry forgers in the world live in Hong Kong. Real artists, who can recreate designer pieces for a fraction of the cost. Their work can fool everyone at a glance—except a jeweler who knows his business. Krakower would have spotted these as fakes the moment she handed them over."

"So where are the real ones?" the cop asked Felicia.

"I have no idea what you're talking about," she said innocently. She gave an exaggerated shrug.

"*That*'s the bad acting I recognize!" Reese said. He turned back to Maggie. "You said she wasn't acting before."

"She said she was scared of what would happen if she lost the earrings. Scared of what her boyfriend would say. Said he would kill her, figuratively speaking, if she didn't return the missing pieces.

That was all true. That was her motive. That was the whole reason for this crazy game we've been playing all night."

She smiled at him. "She was using you, just like you said. She pushed you to invite her to this party, Reese, but not to further her career. She needed to set up this robbery tonight, because she was running out of time to very publicly 'lose' the earrings so she wouldn't have to return them to their rightful owner."

"You can't prove any of this," Felicia said.

"Of course I can. You intended for some innocent person you didn't even know to take the fall for the crime, just to get you off the hook with your ex-boyfriend. In the meantime you'd also have the money you got from selling the real earrings on the black market in Hong Kong."

"You can't charge me with anything," Felicia said.

"She's right," Lieutenant Ibarra said with a sigh. "Unfortunately."

"What about filing a false police report?" Maggie asked.

"She hasn't signed a complaint yet. It's going to be hard to prove."

"You could sue for slander," Maggie said to Abby, but she shook her head.

"I just want to go home," she said.

Maggie started to argue with them, but Reese stopped her. "They're right. There's nothing we can do here."

"Maybe not here," Maggie said. "But I can call Best Jewelers tomorrow and tell Daniel about this, and he can go after her for stealing his jewelry."

"Wouldn't work," Reese said.

"I suppose not," Maggie said. "He wouldn't want his wife to find out, so he'll probably let her get away with it."

"No. It wouldn't work because Daniel doesn't have standing to file a complaint against her." Reese grinned. "I said I'd known his family for years. Nora, my manager, is really good friends with Debbie Best."

"Nora's really good friends with everybody, but who's Debbie Best?"

"Debbie Best Krakower," Reese said. "Owner of Best Jewelers. Didn't you know? Daniel's only an employee. He works for his wife's family business."

"And Debbie Best would be quite willing to call the cops about the loss of her merchandise," she said, the light dawning.

"Yeah," he said. "And I think Daniel will be willing

to testify about what really happened once Debbie has finished with him."

Felicia began to sputter. "But—but—wait—"

"Bye, Felicia," Reese said.

"SHE LEFT," MRS. QUEEN SAID A LITTLE WHILE LATER. "Burned rubber pulling away," she added with a smirk. "Right in front of Lieutenant Ibarra, so I think she's going to hear about that."

Maggie laughed.

"You're that movie star," Abby was saying to Reese.

"His body double," he said. "You can tell us apart because he's an egotistical jerk, and I'm sweet as pie."

"Yeah, right," the girl said. "I don't care who you really are. You stuck up for me when you didn't have to. Thank you."

She held out her hand and he shook it. "You're welcome," he said, and seemed genuinely touched.

Abby gave Maggie a big hug. Then she backed away. "Oh. I'm sorry if I wrinkled your fancy dress."

"Don't worry about it," Maggie said. "I don't care about being fancy."

Jasper circled around the group. He was thrilled

to have a job, bumping them with his hip to keep his herd of people together.

Jasper bumped the petite teenager, almost knocking her over. "And is this Lassie?" she asked.

"Her body double," Maggie said, and they all laughed.

But Abby still seemed a bit sad, and Mrs. Queen said, "it's all over, miss. You don't have to worry anymore."

Abby nodded. "I'm glad I'm not going to get arrested. But I still got fired. I'll have to find a new job right away."

"They fired you?!" Maggie said. "But not after your name has been cleared. Surely they'll take you back."

"No. The temp agency said I caused trouble and they don't want me back."

"Of course they did," Reese muttered, patting his tuxedo pocket for his phone. "I'll talk to them."

But Maggie put up her hand. "Don't worry about it." She turned to the girl. "They'll always treat you disrespectfully. You deserve better than that."

"Respect doesn't pay my tuition," Abby said. "I've got to have a job."

"But I've got a better job for you. Flexible hours, and it's right in downtown Carita. Probably won't pay any more than the temp job, but you'd work for a truly lovely woman. The salt of the Earth."

"What do you mean?" Abby asked.

"There's a new bead shop going in on the main drag in Carita. Across from the coffee house, in an old barber shop that's sitting empty. The shop has a job opening for a part-time clerk, someone who can work there between classes and on weekends."

"But I don't know anything about beads."

"I don't know how to act," Reese said. "And look how far I got."

"And I don't know anything about running a bead shop," Maggie said. "But we'll figure it out as we go."

"Okay," Abby said, smiling for the first time. "Okay. I'd love that."

"Maggie," Reese said when Mrs. Queen took Abby to the buffet for a big plate of prime rib, "is this the wrong time for me to point out that you don't own a bead shop?"

"I will tomorrow. Right after I talk to my husband over breakfast." She grinned. "I think that's the least I should get in the divorce settlement, don't you?"

MAGGIE HEADED DOWN THE LONG STAIRWAY TO THE beach, with Jasper sticking close by her side and Reese bringing up the rear.

The party roared on behind them. The crowd mingled, making deals, frantically celebrating at the top of their lungs, all either genuinely oblivious, or pretending to be, that a marriage had ended tonight, that a kid had almost lost her future over a false accusation tonight, that most of them would go home alone to start it all over again tomorrow.

Maggie took off her Manolos when they reached the beach. The sand was cool and silky beneath her feet, and she didn't care that the hem of her silver gown would never be the same after this. There would be no place to wear this kind of dress in the new life she was about to begin.

They walked out to where a dark line marked where the sand met the sea.

Maggie sat down on the sand just above the tide line. Jasper plopped down next to her on one side and rested his long, bony head on her knee. She petted him absently from nose to forehead, and he sighed contentedly.

Reese sat down on her other side. The hems of his tuxedo pants were covered in powdery sand.

"He didn't deserve you," Reese said.

"We made our choices and we have to live with them, remember?"

"So what's next?"

"Next I'm going to stop wearing high heels. And I'm quitting the fruit juice diet so I can eat everything that's left on the buffet table." She pulled off the fake nail that had been snagging all night. "And I'm going to cut my nails short so I can hold the needles when I do my beadweaving."

"Good for you." He watched the sea. "But it's a nice house. It's a shame to give it up."

"I'm not giving it up. We had a prenup. He cheated, so I get a house. I'll take Casablanca."

They watched the water for a while. "Our tenth anniversary would have been January fifth," Maggie added softly.

"I'm sorry," Reese said.

She cocked her head to listen to the laughter in the house at the top of the cliff. From here the sounds were faint, fading away in the face of the ocean's deep rumble. "I guess I don't feel much like celebrating," she said.

"You can celebrate with me," he said. "Tonight is my eleventh anniversary."

"You're not married."

"Nope. I'm sober."

"Wow. For eleven years."

He stared at the water, but saw something a million miles away. "Eleven years ago tonight I took my last drink of whisky, shot up my last speedball, and slit my wrists."

She shivered at the brutality of the simple words, trying to imagine the desperation that drove someone to that low point.

He watched the sea, and she watched his magnificent profile, chiseled by the moonlight like a Greek god's. She knew the official story. He had started as a teenage rock star all those years ago. Toured and partied and followed the drugs down a rabbit hole until it all ended when he crashed into a tree on Christmas Day, with his whole band in the car with him. He'd killed the guitar player and ruined all their lives. And worst of all, his bandmates had been his best friends since childhood. A week later Nora had found him just in time to keep him from succeeding in that suicide attempt. It had been a long battle back to sobriety, back to stardom—but back to happiness? She wasn't sure about that.

"It's been a long trip," he whispered.

"And look at you now," she said. "Clean, sober, and full of yourself."

"Yeah." He flashed a grin. "Look at the two of us

now. Two regular kids who made it to the top." He leaned back and gazed up at the stars. He added in a whisper, "if I'd died eleven years ago, I would have missed half the journey."

"I'm glad you stayed, Stanley."

"That may be the nicest thing anyone's ever said to me. I'm glad I stayed, too."

He slapped his thighs and stood up. "I'm really glad." He reached out a hand to her and lifted her to her feet.

The stars were icy overhead, as cold and meaningless as the diamond earrings she wore. She fingered them thoughtfully. "I wonder how many beads I can buy with these," she muttered.

He laughed, the famous laugh that this time seemed filled with real joy. "Listen," he said.

The crowd back in the house was counting down: "five, four, three, two, one!"

Then shouting and music.

But there on the sand, with the indigo sea whispering in front of them, all was peaceful, with the big dog leaning his hot, furry body against her thigh, and the tall man standing silently in the darkness next to her.

He leaned down and brushed her lips with a quick kiss, a platonic one, to greet the new year.

She laughed.

"What?"

"I do have something to celebrate," she said. "A new year. A new start. The journey's not half-over yet."

"Happy New Year, Magdalena," he said.

"Happy New Year, Stanley. Let's make it a good one."

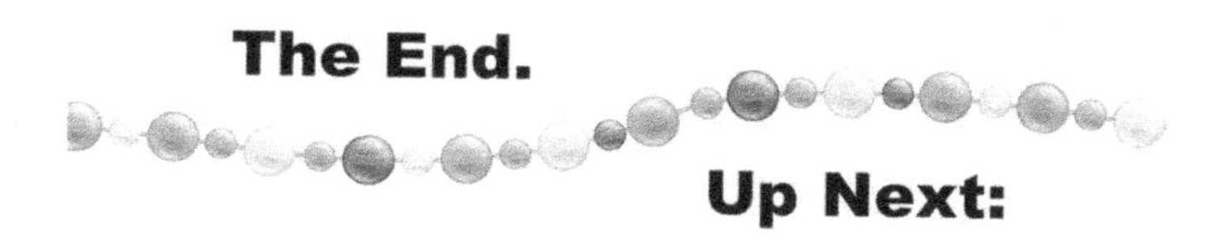

Maggie's got a handsome movie star in her kitchen, a bead shop downtown... and a dead body in the swimming pool. Her new year may not be working out quite like she planned.

She thought starting over would be simple. But there are a few roadblocks on the road to happiness for Maggie and her friends—including that rather inconvenient corpse. Can she figure out who's behind the murder before the killer strikes again?

You can find out now with the first **full-length novel** in the Carita Cove series, ***Maggie and the Inconvenient Corpse***.

Tucker (the real "Jasper")

My favorite pic of the big boy. –Barb

The Carita Cove Mysteries

Maggie McJasper is starting over in a little California beach town. She has a craft shop, a nice circle of friends, and a handsome movie star who keeps flirting with her. Life would be pretty great if she could just stop stumbling over dead bodies....

Maggie and the Black-Tie Affair

A bored trophy wife. A cynical movie star. One evening to save an innocent girl from prison. None of them will ever be the same after this Black-Tie Affair.

Maggie and the Inconvenient Corpse

A handsome movie star in her kitchen, and a corpse in the swimming pool. Just your typical Monday morning.

Maggie and the Mourning Beads

Can Maggie find the real killer when her teenage student threatens to strangle her mother with a jet-black necklace... hours before the woman is found dead?

Maggie and the Empty Noose

When the handsome movie star renting Maggie's house is accused of murder, she's the only one who believes he's innocent. Now all she has to do is prove it.

Maggie and the Huichol Homicide

Maggie searches for the gifted young artist who created an amazing beaded skull–and finds a dead body in her apartment. Can she track down the real killer before someone else bites the dust?

Maggie and the Whiskered Witness

Maggie's dog-training buddy drops off her German Shepherd for a play date–then disappears. Soon Maggie begins to wonder if her friend could be leading a deadly double life.

The Pajaro Bay Mysteries

WELCOME TO PAJARO BAY, THE LITTLE CALIFORNIA beach town where the cottages are cute, the neighbors are nosy, and it's always possible to find your personal Happily Ever After. The novels can be read in any order, or follow along from the beginning to see how the world develops:

HONEYMOON COTTAGE

A tiny beach town, a handsome sheriff, and a chance for a fresh start. Sure, there's a serial killer on the loose, but no place is perfect, right?

BOARDWALK COTTAGE

Hallie thought she'd spend a fun summer at a funky old amusement park. She didn't expect to become the key to solving a kidnapping plot!

LIGHTHOUSE COTTAGE

Alone at a lighthouse with a handsome, sweet… murderer? Lori had better figure out what he's hiding before they both end up as shark bait.

. . .

Little Fox Cottage

Deliver a dog to its new owner, they said. It'll be easy, they said. They didn't say anything about murder.

Rum Cake Cottage

Roxy spent 10 years in prison for a crime she didn't commit. Now she's got 72 hours to find the real killer, or she'll lose her daughter forever.

Songbird Cottage

The abandoned cottage with her grandmother's portrait on the wall is the first clue. Will Robin find the others before it's too late?

Sunshine Cottage

Witness protection in a small town. If Teresa's cover is blown, she'll lose the best life she's ever known. Oh, and she'll die. That, too.

BARBARA COOL LEE WRITES THE kind of books she likes reading: fun and heartwarming romantic mysteries where the good guys treat people with kindness and you can always count on a happy ending.

She lives in a cozy cottage by the sea on the California coast. While she's writing her next book, she's got a loaf of sourdough bread in the oven, a pot of veggie soup on the stove, and the fog is billowing outside the windows.

Be sure to sign up for her newsletter to get all the free short stories and be first to find out when the next book is released.

CPSIA information can be obtained
at www.ICGtesting.com
Printed in the USA
BVHW031036071119
563173BV00001B/157/P